CHRONO TALES

BY

NEILS AXT

Published by Nakxkan Media

Contact:
neilsaxt@gmail.com and
http://www.neilsaxt.com

January 2013

ISBN 978-0-9884520-2-2

For Linda

Thanks for showing us
The beauty of reading

TABLE OF
CONTENTS

Chip Off The Old Rocker

In the distance, a slight rumbling could be sensed, then felt, and then heard. A small animal crouched down in an apprehensive stare out over the hills toward the peak in the distance. Several insects who were buzzing around the kitchen area became silent. Toward Herculaneum nothing seemed unusual. Calm trees were momentarily jostled by a slight trembling in the ground. Animals scurried about, some aimlessly. For a few moments everything, all birds, all animals, everything except the kids playing by the well became silent, as if a hesitation had permeated the land and the sky. At first, none of the people seemed to notice. Soon all sensed the stillness, and began to view each other with a feeling of strange apprehension.

Other feelings were sensed, some subconsciously. Very low frequency vibrations began to slowly touch the perception of those within sight of the mountain. The ground became unstable as if turning to liquid or a gel. Instinctively, all animals, humans included, lowered their centers of gravity a bit by bending their knees. And then it stopped. All living creatures looked around apprehensively as if there were something to see, or more to feel.

Nothing.

At the well, the talk was of 'the feeling' and what it might have meant. Some thought it was an omen, maybe a sign that more would shake, or that it could be simply a momentary adjustment of some kind, of no consequence. The older ones wondered if it was like stories they had heard, about exploding mountains, but that all seemed too far from possible truth, and so was not repeated seriously. People went on with their lives, at least for the moment.

Later that same day Vesuvius exploded with the initial result that a shock wave hit, followed by a quick vacuum pulled on the surrounding area. With the initial pull, all life was swayed toward the mountain for a split second, just before the death wave hit, killing everyone.

The force and heat of the final wave was so powerful that when it arrived nothing could survive. In it was the top half of the mountain, pulverized and mixed with the core of the volcano. It was a mobile form of rock in between a solid and a gas, burning hot enough to obliterate all it hit either by force, or by heat, or by momentum, but not by fear. It was too fast for that. People were blown back by the wave, and then incinerated instantly. Only solid rock survived, but slabs of stone standing upright were also blown down upon each other.

Strange things happened, much as sometimes happens with tornadoes, where force exerted in such a unified direction alters some things almost inexplicably in one single aspect. Window aperture shapes were thereby imprinted by the blast upon rock faces that were behind them in almost the exact way film in original photography was exposed by light. There was, however no film development stage to the process, just the exposure of death through power. There were imprints on some of the rocks that later survived thousands of years. It was the forensic evidence of what had happened, the evidence that would so many years later prove the unbelievable story I am about to tell.

There are strata of understanding, threads of ideas that can transcend time and space. I know of just such a tale, and I must tell it before I am once again at the end of my current life. Now I am an old lady, in a place where the old people are placed when there are sufficient anomalies with them to make them difficult to maintain, or when they cannot maintain themselves. I actually prefer it here, for as I am sitting in the hall, surrounded by others in wheel chairs, staring at the floor, I too am staring, but it lets my mind be free enough to again collect my thoughts, those thoughts that span the millennia. And it is not objective history I keep behind my eyes, but experience, I am a recurring subjective actor in this story over time.

Transduction it might be called, where one event induces into an inanimate object a pattern of information that is cohesive enough to be detected at some later time, to be sensed or to afford perception of sense.

I was transduced, and I only learned about it by accident. Once it became clear what had happened, I was able to reconstruct the information chain, the succession of sensations that occurred over time, much time.

Once, during a magician's show, I was seated with my friends in a night club, and the next act came out, The Psychic Karloff. Karloff asked everyone in the place to write on a slip of paper their first name and one thing that used to keep coming into their minds as children. I wrote "Angie - Volcanoes" and put the slip of paper under the candle on the table as instructed. Later in the show, Karloff announced it was time to see what was under some of the candles, all still at their respective tables.

"Is there a person in the room who wrote something about dreaming of coffins?" he asked. "No, there is more clarity. Something about James, with parents in coffins," Karloff announced. "James, would you please stand up?"

To our amazement, an elderly man stood up by a table across the room and said: "It is I. I am James."

Karloff asked him nothing more, but told him: "It appears you were afraid of losing your parents and that they were already in coffins. A recurring dream I believe, and one that finally did come true, but long, long after you were a child," he said with confidence.

James looked down at the floor, and softly said: "It is true. I hated the dreams and finally forgot them. When you asked us to write something that nobody could possibly know, I thought of that tonight. And I haven't thought of that in fifty years."

The crowd murmured in amazement and Karloff asked the man to sit back down. Several people in the audience quietly commented, that it must have been prearranged, there being no good explanation for how the man could have such perception powers.

I was next. Karloff posed the question: "I can feel that there is someone in the audience who wrote something about "Ann, or Hannah, and then something about mountains, no, explosions, no, Vesuvius... Ann or Annie? Would you please stand up?"

Nobody moved. Karloff continued: "Is it not Ann or Hannah, Anna or Annie maybe?

One of the other people at my table glanced her eyes at me, knowing my name, and wondering if it could be me. I faltered, looked down, then around, and finally rose to my feet, saying nothing.

"Is that you?" asked Karloff, and without waiting for a response, continued his description of the impressions he was apparently receiving about me. "You have not lived before, I believe, but I sense your spirit has. It is rare for me to get such a strong impression, but I can tell there is more to come from your history, some other coincidence, and it may happen here tonight."

"Please tell us your first name, your age and year of your birth, and where you come from, if you don't mind," requested Karloff.

"I am Angie, and I was born in 1932, in England, and I am 64 years old, now living in Ohio," I said quietly.

"And what exactly did you put on your card this evening and why?" asked Karloff.

"I wrote that I have experienced instantaneous death, and by explosion" I said, "though I am not entirely certain why I wrote that. It is more a feeling than a complete thought."

"With your permission, I would like to suggest that we put you in a relaxed state and ask you some things about your past, or shall I say your pasts. I can promise you we will not invade your current privacy, and that we will not make you do anything silly while you are relaxed," said Karloff, starting to talk in a much more soothing and softer tone.

"That is fine, but I am not sure what it is exactly you think you will find. I am not even sure I can relax that much," I said.

At that point Karloff started to talk me into a state where I didn't know exactly if I was asleep or awake. There was a reporter from the local radio station doing a story on Karloff, who was recording the performance in order to analyze it. It is only from that recording that I later pieced together all that happened in those next ten minutes and what it all meant.

After several soothing minutes of repetitive sentences from Karloff, I apparently was open to questions, with eyes closed and able to hear and discuss concepts bypassing my conscious mind.

Karloff began the discussion: "You wrote something about death and explosion. Can you describe any more about that kind of feeling?"

"I was standing in a doorway, but not a modern one. A doorway that was always open with a vertical stone in front of it, more like a walkway than a closing door. We live near Herculaneum, within sight of Vesuvius. There was a strange silence just now and then the mountain explosion. That is all I remember," I said.

Later, from the recording of the session, I learned that I was unconsciously fondling the small rock on the necklace around my neck throughout the interview.

"Where did you get that nice necklace? You seem to like it a lot," Karloff asked.

"My father made a trip in about 1920 before I was born and brought a souvenir piece of rock from an excavated house. I never take it off," I said.

Karloff asked me to hold the piece of stone firmly, and to try and remember what else might be imprinted on it, anything else sense-able.

"Today was a strange morning as I remember," I started. "Though it began as any other, there were some rumblings from the mountain, then everything got very quiet. It was as if the animals were not there anymore. After a while the rumblings got louder and then the large explosion knocked us all down. I remember being covered with rocks and then nothing more," I said.

"Do you realize that explosion happened almost two thousand years ago?" Karloff asked.

"It just happened, just now," I said. "I remember being knocked off my feet and feeling as if my entire existence had been pushed onto the soft rock of the wall. It was only a minute or two ago!"

Karloff gently talked me out of my trance and told me of the things that we had witnessed and discovered. It was not until much later that I was able to piece together the apparent transference of images and personality traits onto a piece of rock that later I was able to detect.

After the evening, several people asked me if I worked for Karloff, as they were certain there was absolutely no way such things could happen.

My only answer was, and has since been, that there are more things contained in the word universe than we can possibly understand.

Since that day, I have had an avid interest in Pompeii but have never succeeded in reviving the ability to decipher more from the rock I wear around my neck.

Karloff died within a year or so after that and this story was included in his biography as one of the strangest of all he ever witnessed.

I now live alone in Cincinnati.

I am 80 years old in the year 2012.

Solid

The night before had been all too familiar for Jim. Same sad, predictable actors and setting. Even the finale held no elements of surprise. In absolute analysis the players were wearied by their roles, not realizing one slight change of direction could alter the intersection of them both forever.

Jimmy and Judie were the perfect match. Everybody knew it. And they were the first, arriving at frightly matrimonial junction long before their high school classmates had seriously considered such options. Everybody knew of their story and their happiness.

But infinitesimal fractures had begun to emerge, compounding over time, so their emotional involvement was in danger of a major quake. So far, there had been only mistakable tremors. But the rumblings continued to frighten. With each disappointment came more doubt. It was grand, that none of the emotional triggers was connected with a firearm...

Last night, this time, Jim and Judie had argued once more about how to pay the bills. But that was not the fundament. It had not surfaced this last time. There was the underlying, repetitive thread about not being able to afford having a child. That too was not the problem; it was that Jim at his epicenter did not feel able to bring another into the world he then knew. He wanted the difference, the delta, some dramatic change from the current before he could replicate.

Judie was not giving up, and kept reminding him, it seemed like every day. It was downright embarrassing to Jim, and was first on his mind as he pulled up at the cement plant at five thirty that next morning. It was still dim and hushed outside. No birds yet sang that day.

"Hey Jim, looks like you got your truck running again," said the foreman as Jim walked in the scheduling shed.

"Yea. Had to replace a U joint after the drive shaft dropped out. Was plum wore out," said Jim with a half smile. Jim was a quiet man, at least until it came to some of the late night arguments, but it took a lot of friction for him to voluntarily emit a sound, especially in social settings. The strong, silent type.

A couple other drivers started coming in for their routes, and on the top of the assignment board was: "25 Loads Today Boys!", which meant all the cement truck drivers would be once again endlessly articulating the trip from plant-to-foundation-pit where a new apartment high-rise was going in. It also meant Jim would get home after dinner again, and the arguments with Judie would fire back up.

Jim grabbed the load list and went to his cement truck. He would end up making four or five loads during the day, all to the same place, and mostly by the same route. Each truck had a number, but all the paint jobs were so worn you could only tell which truck it was by the number painted inside on the dash. Truck 12 was his.

The sound of the cement mixing plant filled the air, as each truck pulled up to be impregnated with its load of liquid stone. Jim was first in line, with nobody behind him. He pulled up, hopped out, and helped the loader fill the truck, then jumped back into the cab of truck 12 for the half hour trip to the construction site.

Out on the road he started thinking of Judie again, and thought about calling her up to say he was sorry about having to miss dinner, but he realized she would not even be awake yet, so he decided to wait until later in the trip for the call.

The site was in an older section of town, at one time residential, later having evolved into part of the very seedy, the 'almost downtown'. Some of the old houses had been changed into restaurants and shops. During the last couple of decades there had been an influx of drugs and crime, a typical inner-city problem. But the construction site had obliterated about fifteen blocks of the problem and was about to get a much more stable foundation.

Jim turned off onto 12th street and was about four blocks from the site. He usually took the 10th street cut-through, which was shorter, but he wanted to break things up. And that section was part of a quaint area renovated a decade earlier. Besides, he was thinking about Judie. He had the cement truck stopped at the three-way by the old bridge, and a new, bright blue German convertible came quickly down the side street, while he was stopped at the stop sign. The BMW didn't stop at the sign, barely slowed down, dispensing with even a "rolling stop". The convertible swerved up the wrong side of the intersection around him.

"Hey Jackass! Get the hell out of the way would ya? Get a job and make some money," shouted the short bald man in the convertible. The top was down, so Jim could see inside just fine. As the car sped by, Jim saw the license plate with "HI$ TOY" on the back.

It was still almost completely dark outside. Jim slowly got the massive momentum of his truck moving up the street by going through the gears. At the next cross street was a coffee shop built into an old house. Several cars and minivans were parked along the street down a block or so, and the bright blue convertible was a good six cars back from the intersection. He saw the same license plate.

Just then, Jim remembered having seen the car, and the person before. In the last couple of weeks there had been a driveway pour job at an enormous house on the north side. It was the house for this same guy, and Jim remembered how the foreman, and the drivers had been chided and berated by the man. Mostly there were only silly comments about how dumb the country music was the truckers listened to.

Calmly, Jim pulled the cement truck alongside the convertible and got out, walking around to the delivery controls by the chute. Pulling the chute over so it was right over the top of the BMW, Jim started whistling that country song about "Being Nice is Better Than Being Right..."

When the chute was centered, Jim pulled the dump lever so the cement started flowing down into the fine German car. Jim knew the capacity of his truck as well as he knew how many beers he could hold. And one convertible's worth of cement would never be missed at the site. As the cold molten rock slithered onto the perfect leather seats onto the custom floor mats, he made a quick calculation in his head. If the interior had a width of, say, four feet, and a length of five, that's twenty. And if it's about two feet high that would be about forty cubic feet of the incoming gray. At about a hundred pounds per cubic foot that would be an almost instantaneous addition of three or four thousand pounds to the car.

It only took about two minutes for enough cement to flow into the car up to the windows. Over those two minutes, the change was dramatic. Loud popping sounds came from the suspension as it tried to withstand an unsustainable load. Some sounded like gun shots. Others creaked and groaned. Finally, the car squatted down as it put on the weight, not unlike the unfortunate aspect ratio of a fat person who looks wider than tall.

The low-profile performance tires got lower as cement settled around leather seats. Tire rims pushed down through rubber, cutting through down into the asphalt, easing the car lower where the lacerated rubber of the tires gave way. Springs and suspension compressed to let the body down on the road. Solid German doors started bulging out, but did not break.

Inside, the interior was now filled with cement and Jim stopped the flow, pulled the chute back, and calmly as ever, got into his truck and drove to the site.

"Hey Jimmy! First load of the day?" shouted the foreman when he got there.

"Yea, looks like it will be a quiet one."

Jimmy just smiled, and said: "Yup."

Washed Up

In a small old southern town like the one where Esther lived there was no reason not to know everybody's business. At the Rexall drug store on Main Street there was no secrecy, though there was certainly the maintenance of the direct social idea of propriety as customers came in to get their personal things, with no real cause for alarm. Everybody usually knew everybody, and their relations, their stories and problems, including ills, remedies, tries and failures, not that any of that was ever mentioned from behind the smiles.

Often, there a plausible story line would accompany those who came through the drug store door, as happened the time when several teenagers discovered poison ivy in the meadow by the dump. Several of them coming in for some calamine lotion to rub on their backs. Nobody outwardly mentioned just how they could have gotten such a thing on their backs of course, but the incident was duly noted with requisite repetition at the barber shop over by the newspaper typesetter's office.

Esther didn't go to the barber shop, and when she did go by the drug store she made sure she didn't pass on any real intelligence, as she knew the rules of social engagement as well as anyone. Some ladies were not so discriminating, preferring to reap and sow informational tidbits wherever and whenever they could, not timid about introducing distortions of opinion along the way. All the more engaging then that the tale of Esther's new car should make the rounds without her even knowing.

It all started when Esther's son Ron came for a visit and found her car inoperable. He started a campaign to replace it, a full-force research-and-sales effort with Esther to make sure she knew her independence was at stake, and that having a vehicle was a requirement, not an option, of living alone. Besides, it was 1962 and just about everybody bought a new car every other year anyway.

Ron had seen the pictures of the new Chevy station wagons and simply wanted to see for himself. It was a hot summer day when he rode over to Miller's Chevrolet over by the old Borden condensed milk plant. Old man Miller was not there, but one of his sons showed Ron the new station wagons, and the Nova model, describing several features, like the powerful 283 engine under the hood. Since there was no sense in trying to get Esther a station wagon, no matter how much Ron would love her to have one, he decided to take a Nova for a spin. Small car, nice V8 under the hood, and a gravel patch by the tracks made him forget he was test driving it for his mother.

"This thing"ll sure skeedaddle. Don't let her get away from ya," said one of the Miller boys along for the ride.

"Jimmy Butler laid a streak o' rubber out on the county road by the lake musta' been a quarter mile long with one of these things. Has a four-barrel carb and you can feel it right?" He obviously loved it. "Kick you back like a rocket. I tell you I love this job. I get to run the piss out of these things and then, oh, uh, I mean, we do test drive them a bit when they come in," he said, realizing passion had trumped discretion.

Ron circled back to the dealership and parked right in front of the big glass window. "Real nice car. Would like to get one for my Mom. She needs something since her old Dodge died, though I still would want to trade that in," he said. "I will bring her in to see your dad soon as I can."

The Dodge was worthless and they both knew it, but it was going to be a part of any deal, when and if it came to that. Of course Esther barely needed a car at all and she certainly didn't need a V8, but then that really didn't matter. What mattered was that she had something, and that it would be fun to buy a car. And besides, Ron was only in town for a week before he would have to head back home, and that six-hour drive over would be no fun if he was always worried she couldn't get around by herself. And besides, it was important for Esther to feel independent too, and to have something to do and to talk about. Ron went back to the house his Dad and Esther had built, and found Esther there as usual, watching endless news and weather on the TV.

He decided to take her out to dinner.

"How about we go to the buffet place tonight, what's it called Clyde's?" he asked when he had washed up. "And after that we can drive through the university to see the new dorm they are working on." Ron knew any excuse to take a ride and talk would be welcome. Esther went to her room to start getting dressed. "Should we call Marguerite?" she asked.

There were friends, and then there was Marguerite. Later in life, when none of the ladies could remember a sentence, they would sit in the senior care center, looking at each other during the lunch, knowing they shared some history, but neither one really wanting to talk, or they would remember the way life used to be, with more light than dark, more passion than not, and no worry of finality. In this earlier time, though, there still were a few of the ladies in the Sunday school class Esther would see out and about on occasion. She welcomed an excuse, any excuse, to brush her teeth, put on some clothes, and go for a ride.

They got to Clyde's and ate the overcooked southern vegetables from the buffet, all prepared by the enormous black ladies in the back, under the dictatorship of Clyde, whose only claim to fame was about five years in a U.S. Army kitchen. Southern fried 'everyprotein' accompanied the spread, as did the various sugar-laden desserts of dough-intensive cobblers, with canned-fruity goodness in sickly-sweet profusion.

"Went over to Miller's Chevrolet today for a test ride in one of those little jobs, the Nova. Nice tight little ride. I'm thinking it would be perfect for you, since your Dodge is about done. I want to make sure you have something you can count on to get to Sunday school and of course the aerobics classes over at the hospital," Ron noted, during pudding and cobbler. "It's important you can trust your car, especially since I am the closest in the family and I am living so many hours away now."

Esther swirled her chocolate pudding with her fork, and then said: "You sure I need something that nice? If Daddy were here he could have kept the Dodge going for sure, and with almost no new parts. It's not the money you know, you are probably right, but I need a car so little. If I didn't live outside of town it wouldn't be worth it."

Ron knew he had her. It was like the old days when he would want to get permission for something and he would set up the sequence in his mind of things he would mention, and when and about how long it would take to convince her of his viewpoint. But now that she was alone, the talks were always easier. And the feeling that she had plenty of money for her needs made it even simpler.

"You know, what we could do tomorrow on the way to the grocery store is go by Miller's and let you try one out. I tell ya', my ride today was real nice. I tried out a grey one but I also saw a bright red model there on the lot you might like," he said. "Let's make it a point to go by and take a test drive."

"Sure," she said, "If you think it's right."

Next day, they went over to Miller's and Esther made Ron drive the red one first, with old Mr. Miller in the tiny back seat. Then Esther agreed to take the wheel, driving first over by the elementary school where she had once taught. Familiar roads, in an unfamiliar setting. She went about twenty five miles an hour and kept her left foot on the brake the whole time. She was the master of burned out brakes, brake jobs, and a silent champion for all repair shops for miles around.

It was a sale.

After Ron had been gone a couple of weeks, and Esther had gotten more comfortable with the car, she would make trips just for fun, to the grocery store mostly, but also through the college campus and around town. During one of those trips she saw an old biplane going overhead, heard it first actually, as it took her back to much younger days when her father was still alive.

"You can hear the cycles in that internal combustion engine," he would say. She thought about him so many times, while driving her new car, she finally did hear it she thought. When an old biplane flew by in the air overhead, she was convinced of it. Her mind kept drifting back to the old days with the family car, the old Ford from the forties, while she rode out by Gentry's store in the new red Chevy.

After a couple of minutes she started listening to the new engine in her car, and finally thought she heard some strange sound, a kind of ticking or clacking sound. Couldn't be certain it was the engine but somewhere in the car she could tell a sound had changed, sufficiently enough that she decided to ride on over to Miller's and have them take a look at it. As she pulled up in front of the showroom old man Miller was just getting to work himself, and noticed her drive up.

"Hey Esther!", he said with a big smile on his face. "How is that Nova working out for you?"

"I love it, John," she said, "but you know, there is a strange sound developing, I am certain of it. Noticed it today riding out by Gentry's and I wanted you to hear it. Reminds me of those old biplane engines. You could hear something in the engine," she said as they walked in the showroom.

"Well, Esther, I don't want you ever to hesitate coming back on in here whatever you hear in that car. We will make it right. Let me have somebody take it in the back and get it tightened up for you. You want a Dr. Pepper or something while you wait?" he said as he smiled.

"Oh no thanks. I am on my way to lunch with Marguerite, but thanks all the same," she said as she sat down in the showroom, with her purse on her lap.

Old man Miller went back into the shop where his sons were sitting around talking and said: "Esther is back boys, and she is hearing sounds again just like before. Thinks she knows when she hears some sort of airplane engine sound."

"Should we check the front end again or something?" asked one of the boys.

"You think something is wrong with it this time?"

"Nope. Just give it a wash and put it back out front for her right quick would ya?"

"Give it a wash boys, just a wash."

Slice of Life

Talent is where interest lives. Curiosity yields an endless variety of individuals, recombined from the sums and differences of the parents. Chance allows for the creation of an almost infinite number of populous combinations. It is like an artist mixing paints, this genetic sorcery, there can never be an exact match. If there were an earthquake in the paint mixing room it might be an appropriate corollary for what goes on during the millisecond when the chance sperm meets target egg. It is amazing then, that more don't turn out like our principal player at the moment, Mr. Christian Kohler, junior.

Before he knew what was happening, Christian was living in Denmark as a child, with his Danish Mother in a part of Copenhagen, not far from Valby. His Mother's apartment was up exactly seventy one well-worn stairs to the third floor. It had always intrigued Christian; there were twelve steps per flight, each flight except the last. And he counted them every time he went up or down. It was his talent for analysis at work. Sometimes he would purposefully not turn on the hall light timers so he could count the steps, make the turns in the dark and do it all from memory, ending perfectly at that top seventy-first step.

Herr Kohler, senior, had moved out of his end of their apartment and back to Germany, taking the little red four-door VolksWagen that had been parked so long in the street, gathering tickets. Not that it was worth much anyway. But he figured he had to win at something out of the last couple of years. Up until then they had tried to stick it out in order to give Christian a fighting chance. In the end, each declared a truceful victory and agreed to end the war. There had not been enough luck in the entire country of Denmark to keep Herr Kohler from miserably failing. His argument had been that motorcycle mechanics were underappreciated there, but in reality he had been lazy, preferring to soak up benefits from the Danish linkage through his wife Ursula and her school-teaching job.

The apartment showed few lasting signs of the father after he left. In truth, he had barely influenced them at all over the years.

Our young character Christian actually started life in Denmark, where the sexual revolution had taken hold and matured before much of the rest of the world could even bring themselves to repeat the words sex and pleasure. Such was the context of life in the sixties and seventies when Christian was a child.

The reader may appreciate what it was like to live through the Danish/Germanic distortion of young Christian's life. Certainly, there are other, many other, reasons for things to have become compromised, the social portrait related here will enable you to fashion for yourself the sequence of events. It is obvious that things evolved, but also they digressed on occasion to form an astounding balance between a life of possible value, and the opposite. Death.

This story is one that makes it impossible to ignore genetics, and understanding of evolutionary programming only now finding its way into the sciences, where there will be breakthroughs in DNA computing. No, what I have to tell you is the story of one who suffered at the hand of God, and at the fingernails of mere mortals who did not know the import of treating each and every creature, including Christian, with the utmost respect.

Life is odd. Lives are strange. The dead are so silent.

It is with infinite humility that I now tell you of the story of Mr. Christian Kohler, the younger, and his predilection for change, the kind of change that makes life appreciate or depreciate. There really is no predicting seeds, women, men, or markets.

Some people are biased toward the inorganic, where they learn and spend their lives working with things inanimate. The interactions, and the methods for working with predictable computers or machines, hold their interest. There are others who prefer the organic, the living, the talking, the blooming, the breathing. Then there are those organic appreciators who fantasize about the organic non-living. The dying. The dead. Our Mr. Kohler fits in that last category, though he had not thought enough about it to have actually known. He simply moved through life without conscious management of thought or action, much as a small cat gets repeatedly distracted and amused by a sound or movement.

Christian constantly observed life forms around him. On the way home one day, riding his bicycle past the IRMA grocery store in his Danish neighborhood, he saw a delivery truck with several trays of peppers and celery being unloaded and stacked on the sidewalk. The deliveryman had spilled something that looked like garlic and Christian noticed as he approached on his bike it was from a tray of beautiful, large mushrooms. The man was picking them up and throwing them back into the truck to later discard. As he worked, he bent way down, doubled over to get them all. Christian was presented with a nearly perfect view of the butt muscles on the man, who was an admirable anatomical combination of youth and vigor. Years of lifting had refined the buttocks and arm muscles to a point no shirt or pants could attempt to conceal the goodness. It was not a sexual impression for Christian, more an appreciation of the physical form, much as an artist appreciates in order to paint a picture.

Christian had never fallen in love. His body and his mind had never been coincident with each other and another. He was virginal in his view and his practice. Every stimulus created a novel response perceived as new, as original, at least to him. Not having experienced anything, so to speak, he was at the mercy of any and all sensations. It was not that he was necessarily gay, or not, or into the occult, or not. It was all the same to him, as he had no frame of reference.

Later that summer, the family decided Christian needed a profession, and he had always shown an interest in cooking and food preparation. The closest opportunity for such work would be at the food store by the apartment, so Ursula and Christian went over to see about employment. There was a course at the nearby trade school, a night course, in food preparation, including the arts & sciences of vegetables, and one about meat preparation. It was decided the first and most useful course would be 'Vegetable Preparation' but there were no openings at that time, so Christian was enrolled in meat and butcher shop essentials.

It wasn't long before Christian started to show his interest in anatomy, and actually exhibited a talent for grasping the intricacies of butchery. Large pieces of beef would arrive in the back of the shop, and the students were instructed in analyzing, naming, and ultimately cutting through the carcasses. They learned how to physically divide meat into portions of steaks, roasts, and other cuts normally found in a grocery store. The tools used were enormous, as with the band saw. The circulating blade was designed to take a slab about the size of one of the students, and cut right through fat, meat, and bone, quickly and cleanly. During the training, constant safety warnings were issued as to the danger of the tools. It was obvious the efficient blade could just as easily and cleanly sever a hand as a piece of chilled beef.

Of most interest to Christian was the training on cutlery. The history of knife making fascinated him. The physics of how knives actually cut was presented, including designs of modern ceramic blades. Microscopic photographs of razors, and knives in various stages of sharpness, dullness, and decay were shown. What interested Christian most was that they were all essentially saws, performing a tearing motion through the flesh. At high magnification even a new surgeon's scalpel could be shown to be comprised of microscopic serrations.

For the first time in his life Christian was sexually aroused, not toward any particular person, but by the prospect of slicing through living flesh, living human flesh, and of knowing that most if not all such cuts would be irreversible, for life, or to the death.

It had not awakened in him the real desire to actually do anything, as that was not his kind of genetic urgency. He intensely enjoyed watching living muscle, especially under stress, and the mechanics of cutting gave him a sense of satisfaction and power, it aroused him. He told no one. He almost couldn't believe it himself. He had a kind of nefarious calling, an alert to a drive he had never imagined, and had not sought.

Each day, after the school sessions Christian would sit on the bench by the bus stop and watch the people stepping up into the buses. The tight, black stocking pants on the girls afforded him better-than-naked, cinematic views of their musculatures. Christian would imagine the physics of the muscles, and how they would instantly change if a knife were somehow pulled across and through, to the bone. He wondered if the person could keep walking at all or would simply fall over. He could imagine all angles of cuts, through tendons, even through bones. But the most interesting to him were cuts through large muscles. He even imagined the change a sharp knife would make into a living heart. At last he was acutely interested in something.

It was about this time when Christian's mother Ursula met another man, an American, and it was decided in a kind of whirlwind that Ursula would move to Georgia in America and live with this Mr. Phil Dawson just outside of Atlanta. Phil lived on the Alabama side of town out where there were large tracts of land and horse farms with plenty of southern to go around.

The choice of joining the new couple in America was left to Christian, who upon hearing the news asked if he could go spend some time in Germany with his father in order to decide. About the middle of March, when winter winds were starting to give way to rains, Christian took the train from Copenhagen through to Germany. During the ferry part of the ride, Christian looked back out on the windmills along the coast of Denmark and wondered if he would ever in his life get back up that far north. There wasn't really any attraction for him now that the entire family had left. But he did have a fond feeling for the school where he had learned that above all one of the great appreciations for him and his talent was anatomy and meat cutting.

After the train cars had been moved onto the ferry for the trip across to Germany, Christian noticed with great interest a young girl who also watched him. He noticed her walking through the second-class cabin on her way toward the train's dining car. She had a thick knit sweater tight enough over her young breasts that Christian found himself appreciating her unconsciously. She gave him a knowing, coy look, trying out her relatively new-found attractiveness in an ongoing experiment to practice and perfect her powers of feminine magnetism. There was far less thought devoted to the potential consummation of the game, and more cunning and cultivation of the non-linguistic interplay. They exchanged stimuli. It was a silent give and take, a mutual acknowledgment.

The exchange of energy in the social game of sexual interaction and stimulus is a communication system, though it is situated much lower than language and more directly connected than other social systems. It links through call and response. It is animal. To use the equation from the much more recently-devised discipline of physics, it is the transfer of energy, the doing of work, the moving of something. The initial transfer is ethereal and cognitive in a lower order. It is informational, it is seminal. It is peremptory. It is pre-semen-al.

Before any tangible, physical agreement, it is the surrogate potential of interaction, that glance, that unmistakable look, and the allowance that it could be misconstrued, or even ignored, or coyly denied. But the showing, the acts of appreciating mutually, the knowing, the willingness, in the mix of every glance, every interaction from young to old, from then to now, is the distillate, the elixir of seduction.

They watched. They mutually appreciated. They made it obvious to each other without words, sound and language unnecessary in those beginning exchanges. Only once did either utter a sound. As she walked by Christian on her way back to reboard her train car, she casually said the German greeting 'Tschuss' as she passed. Christian was too stunned to speak. He never forgot the girl, the voyage, or the heartbreak of not having said anything when he had the chance. It was as if a motorcycle could not move because the engine was vapor locked. It was stasis. He was crushed.

As the train finally pulled into the Leipzig station, Christian started remembering, in reverse, many parts of his life. There were the real problem years when he was a new teen, wasting time behind his father's motorcycle repair shop, listening to stories from an array of patrons, some of whom actually paid for work performed. The largest fraction of attendees and involvees were neither paying constituents nor assisting in any meaningful manner. They were listening to some minimal degree, and were commentators of the most voluminous capacity. This is where Christian's education really began. It's where his appreciation started for things only marginally explicable, and wholly misunderstand-able. It was an environment where concepts were verbally improvised upon, with almost unlimited enhancements and modulations. Size meant status. The bigger and more imposing the presenter, the more respect they received, and the more leeway with the truth that was allowed. There was even more import afforded to any presenter who had the most tattoos, or perforations for accommodating sparkling accouterments, not unlike pygmies in Africa with their penis wraps on and showing.

As always, respect is relative. Aside from size, linguistic powers enforced the motorcycle shop pecking order most dramatically. The more vulgar the language the better, on occasion spiced up even more dramatically by the inclusion of new corruptions learned elsewhere in the proving grounds of prisons and detention centers across Germany. That dark and greasy repair shop was a theater of violence, sometimes self-inflicted.

Christian's father drank himself to gentle sleep each night, sinking down to his knees at first and then at each day's conclusion traversing the finite distance between the upright position of man and the horizontal imposition of sleep. Only time and next-day wakefulness brought evidence the man horizontal on the shop floor was actually alive.

Years later, of course, that horizontal position, half rolled over and half flat on his back, was where the authorities ultimately found him, for once not simply dead to the world but, but finally, insensate, for all of time. It was as if the fatal attraction of earth had finally won the daily argument with the man, pulling him down to his ultimate organic resting place in death.

The shop was ultimately converted to a pool hall, after the city government annexed the building nearby. No one then seemed to remember the theater of characters that had so animated the place there before.

In the couple of weeks it took Christian to decide to move to America with his mother, he received an almost unlimited education while at the shop. Behavior at the place was completely slanted away from what could be considered healthy, but it was alive, seldom restrained, vivid, and exciting. Topics for performance included: street racing, theft, drinking, whoring, fighting and various accounts of doing bodily harm. It was that last inestimable category that most fascinated the mind and talents of Christian, the younger. In excruciating, and often wholly improvised detail, the boy learned from those congregating in his father's shop the theoretical disciplines of firearms, and of more interest to him, of knivery.

"When I was in the slammer, I saw a guy cut up one these little piss-ant boys, you know, the kind that's always going on braggin' or complainin' about somethin' or other. I saw him get pieced apart by an old timer who had nothing but a sliver of stone smaller than a fingernail. He had sharpened it over the years just by rubbin' it and rubbin' it some more against the brick," said the man Thrash. "And didn't nobody told on they guy ever. Far as anybody knew, there wasn't nothin' happened there. Well 'sept that little guy was in pieces."

Thrash was a very large man. Everything about him was large, from his girth to the size of his hands. Well, except for his brain, which had suffered genetically from a quantitative standpoint. Even his cranium was diminutive, making his overall countenance comical, somewhat like a man wearing a tiny hat that is far too small for his head.

Thrash continued to expound at some length about how he had single-handedly outwitted the Leipzig police the summer before during the festival. Everyone knew he was making up the story, but drama sometimes had a life of its own. Each story shared in the shop was modulated by others there who would assist in the embellishment, or sometimes simply refute the entire premise of a tirade. Mostly, these interjections merely altered the course of the story, though sometimes there would be raging arguments and fights.

Christian decided he could always come back to this life and this very shop if he ever wanted to, and so decided to move to America, to Georgia with his mother and forthcoming stepfather. That decision made, he informed his Dad and the others in the shop that he was leaving just as soon as he could make the necessary arrangements. A spirited argument ensued where all in the room shared their personal viewpoints as to the value, or perceived lack of value of that entire undisciplined, undereducated, renegade society, across the ocean.

The plans were made for travel to Atlanta, including the collection of about two hundred dollars in cash for the trip and move. That kind of money was difficult to come by, and in fact, Ursula arranged to purchase the ticket, knowing the financial pressure Christian senior was under. The spending money was arranged in part by some of those friends in the shop donating to the future of the boy.

After Christian had been gone for several months from the area, a startling discovery was made near the motorcycle repair shop. At first there was only a smell, and then the discovery by a tree of two shallow graves. A full-grown, beautiful German shepherd dog was found buried, in two separate places. The animal's legs had been cut off at the joints and buried together a short distance from the main body, covered only by some leaves and branches. It appeared there had been some experimentation with a knife as the legs had multiple cuts around the joints before the final separation.

"Stay behind the line please," urged the airport person as the line of haggled Europeans exuded from the plane, snaking toward baggage claim. It was a time before security guards, so the talent sets of those helping guide the arrivers didn't exactly mean they were fit for that particular job. Unlike in Germany, where jobs were filled with highly educated and trained workers, here it was a kind of randomness that put any one person in a particular position. It had more to do with who showed up to work that day, and at what time, than with talent.

From the moment he landed at the airport, Christian realized it was going to be one interesting voyage into a kind of free-form play of improvisation and experimentation that normally didn't happen in Germany, or Denmark for that matter. In America it was as if rule sets were largely optional. Christian had arrived in America, in Atlanta.

Ursula and Phil met Christian at the Atlanta airport, waiting just behind the yellow line on the floor. Just as soon as they all got in the car, the very first topic was food. And the first and only serious proposal was to immediately head for Betty B'z in downtown Atlanta. That meant BarBQue, and it meant quite an experience. There only three things in that part of town worth mentioning. First, was the old cemetery, the one where Margaret

Mitchell and many other dignitaries had been buried. Margaret promptly got run over in Atlanta by a taxi driver while crossing the street long after completing her book 'Gone With The Wind'.

Another attraction thereby was the open stage art and performance theater known as ShowBall. It was a place where almost anybody could get on stage, perform, be a comedian, and try to win or fail at any other art form. It was wholly improvisational. There were also very inexpensive artworks adorning the walls of the place. The only other distinguishing feature was the pile of free stickers by the door espousing ShowBall as a place where anything could happen. Those stickers did find their way all over creation, making many wonder what ShowBall was, and, due to the omission of any contact information, exactly where.

Across the street from ShowBall and also across from a defunct Greek restaurant was Betty B'z, where the art of meat smoking, and wood burning, and very relaxed cooking met Atlanta. Salient features of the place included open windows, with zip-lock baggies of water hung at the tops. The idea was that prismatic colors refracted from the bags confused flies who came calling for the food smells and so kept them away. Whatever the actual physics behind the things, there were no bugs to be seen despite the lingering smell of smoked pork butt and beef ribs in the air.

Inside, Betty Boyette ran the show. She was large, no, she was enormous, loud, boisterous and happy to see anybody show up, including the police who routinely lined the parking lot due to the 'free meals for cops' program. It did help to make the place look respectable, when there were several police cars parked out front. In reality, it was not much more than a shack.

"You folks are in the right place now. Looks like you could use some of Atlanta's best," Betty said when she saw them all come in. "There ain't no way you're leavin' without also tryin' some of the smoked short ribs. Here, take a taste of that". And she threw a smoked beef rib about big around as a baguette onto the chopping board and sliced some off the side. She put the sliced bits onto a paper towel and set it up on the ordering counter. "Ya'll taste yourselves some of that and then let's see what we got to do about it." She was smiling at them in a friendly, maternal way.

As each one of them took a piece of the meat into their mouths their expressions changed into smiles. Christian said: "What in the world is that? It is great!"

"That's our smoked beef short rib. Smoked sixteen hours, and our special on Thursdays and Saturdays. Nice huh?" The rib was anything but short, at about a foot long at least. But short rib it was called.

Christian said: "Amazing. I will take an order of that myself."

"What two sides you want with that?" asked Betty.

"Sides? What sides means?" questioned Christian with a thick German accent.

"Well honey, you're not from around here are you? Tell you what. I would get the fried okra and then the beans if I were you, or swap one out for the sweet potato french fries," said Betty. "You'll love 'em. And get a big sweet iced tea too, Darlin'. We'll take care of you here. What's your name anyway?"

"I am Christian Kohler from Europe, Denmark and Germany. Christian with a C and Kohler with a K," he said with an obvious accent.

"Well," said Betty. "That's all good. But I am going to call you CK if you don't mind."

Betty sounded black but was so white she seemed to have escaped the sun for her entire lifetime. And the rolling fat under her arms advertised that she was a faithful participant in the barbecue phenom.

A couple of buxom, young, smiling waitresses carried the orders from the back out to the tables, calling out the names of the groups to locate them. One of the girls had a design tattooed all the way up her arm to her ear on her right side.

Ursula, and Phil Dawson ordered and then found a table in the room beyond the bar. A sign on the wall said: "Notice of lost dog. One leg missing. An eye also gone. Not much fur remaining. Answers to the name of Lucky."

Phil started the conversation with Christian. "Glad you're here. I think you'll like Georgia and the culture. It's certainly not northern Europe, like Germany or Denmark, but it has some real nice cultural aspects. Like this BBQ experience. And we have a nice farm out by Villa Rica off the freeway, with a separate building you can probably craft into an apartment down by the barn. It's a block house that was used for milking when the place was a cow farm. Should be pretty comfortable while you figure out what you want to do."

"I work mostly from home as a veterinarian, so I get calls for various things from injured animals to cats with colds. A lot of times, people will come by with their animals, so we have a fridge off from the kitchen with the various drugs and doses I administer. Pretty friendly all around. The house was built in the late 1800s, has a nice breezy covered front porch, and a big barn with silo on the property. By the barn is a good fishing lake and another tool shed where we keep the tractors running," he said, toying with his receipt.

Ursula looked at Christian and said: "We are so glad you decided to come join us here. I think you will love it, and can get a nice clean start here. You can basically do anything you want. It is a lot different than what we are used to. People pretty much leave you alone long as you are not hurting anybody or their stuff. You'll see, there are some great things here."

"And we have an old pickup you can use too. Needs some work, but I know you can get it going. Not much, but it will get you around," Phil said.

Christian looked tired, dazed from the travel, and appreciative. "You are doing great things for me. I appreciate it. I Cannot wait to see the place, and to help pitch in."

The farm had a large white house on a hill, a long covered front porch the whole width of the house, with a winding driveway up from the road. An enormous pecan tree around the side gave shade over a swing from its branches and several seats arranged there beneath. It was there that friends, neighbors, and clients of the animal doctor business usually converged, sooner or later.

A dilapidated tool shed still stood near the house, yielding a nice panorama of the whole scene. Most stunning was a red barn and silo a couple hundred yards away on a hill, behind which was the fishing lake. Horses, goats, chickens, and dogs were all busy neighing, ninnying, crowing, and barking. It was an absolutely beautiful vista. Nearer the lake and by the barn was the white cement block house, the old milking building. It actually looked the newest of them all.

"Welcome to Windy Hill," said Phil as they arrived that first time. "The white building is an old milk barn with electricity and water and all. Could make a nice place to bunk. Or heck, the silo has nothing in it either. Hasn't had anything in it for years. We could probably build some sort of apartment in the top of that thing too if you wanted, but there are no hookups in there. Someday maybe if you want to."

The place really was called Windy Hill on the map, and on a clear day could be seen several hills away the cemetery by the fork in the road. It was also the place Phil's father was buried. A nice breeze seemed to blow almost all the time up across the lake and over the hill with the barns on it.

"Let's get your stuff and get it up the stairs. There is an old bedroom up there in the house you can stay in for now. The closet is just an old gun room, but it'll do," Ursula said and grabbed a couple of things to take in and went up the stairs to the upper bedroom.

The house was a bit stuffy, with no central air conditioning, as usual for the older houses. And the windows were from long ago when tall ceilings and long windows were the style. The panes of glass showed striations and impurities from having been made in a time when glass-making processes were not so standardized as today. Some veterinary supplies were in the kitchen, as well as a Nikon microscope on the counter for analyzing animal samples. Phil worked mostly with dogs, cats and horses. But there were the occasional ferret or turtle to try and help.

Christian settled in well to the place and the life. He lived in the upper room, helping with the animals on the farm. And he became a part of the community. It turned out that Betty Boyette from the barbeque place in town lived a couple of miles away. Betty introduced Christian to a young girl named Jean Ann who was a school teacher at the middle school, a girl who not only had a faithful following of students and teachers, but also a thriving business as a math tutor for many kids. Jean Ann Taylor had a handsome long face, a fetching figure, and limitless youthful energy. Jean Ann complemented Christian with the kind of methodical, sensible, regularized management his personality lacked. Betty had introduced them at the Piggly Wiggly where CK had become the butcher. The job was perfect for him as he was prepared, confident, and doing things that he absolutely loved. He did have to learn some of the local names for cuts of meat, but it was all within the context of his trade. He blissfully created packages like "Center Cut

Bone-In Pork Loin Chops, Family Pack" and Boston Butt's. He even put signs up to catch attention of his service like: "Quality Meats - Sliced Free".

He did very well at work, and enjoyed occasionally interacting with customers, who would ask for various cuts, or how to cook things. Increasingly, Jean Ann would come by to do her shopping when he was working. They would invariably interact, and finally they started dating. In a short time they decided to get married, and the wedding took place at the farm on Wendy Hill. For the reception there was a full spread of BBQ that Phil and Ursula had put together with the help of Betty Boyette. There must have been several hundred well-wishers present, sucking down the free beers and the 'Q'. The event was talked about for years thereafter.

Within a year Jean Ann was pregnant, and there followed two other children. Before long there were kids in the kitchen, helping cook, and wash up. CK started teaching them the functionality of knives, from the microscopic perspective, where they could all be seen as small saw blades, with serrations...He also taught them how to begin using a paring knife, which is somewhat counterintuitive, as the pull is toward one's own thumb.

Often, while in the close quarters of the kitchen, with one of the children, he would have a knife in his hand, and would wonder again for a split second what it would feel like to pull the blade forcefully through a young, living, healthy muscle.

He knew the kinds of force needed, and he was so intimate with the balance between sharpness of a knife and the force that would be required relative to the intended target: muscle, bone, fat, other, that he almost constantly thought of the sensations of actually consummating those thoughts in a life and death action.

The numbers of missing animals and pets in the area around CK and Jean Ann's house increased during those years when their kids were young. Not one person ever equated those disappearances with CK in any way. Only his daughter Anna on occasion would look up into his eyes when he was daydreaming with a knife in his hand, and without preamble ask:

"Daddy? What's wrong?"

Maiden Voyager

Some days are like all days and then no days are really the same, as long as there isn't too much self-focus I suppose. There are several in my family who, if they could contact me now, would be squirming where they are if they knew even a part of the story I am about to relate. Not that there is a way for them to know, as there is no cross-dimensional link, no whisper over the fence, no chat while walking the dogs available to us. This dimensional distortion is less negotiable than the wink of an old man at a young girl. Neither side of the equation knows there is a calculus of life on the other side.

Beautiful day at the outset really, the cool earth, moist ground with the roots of all life being warmed by dancing silhouettes of leaf shadows. Luxurious smells of the sexual flowerings from nearby plants oppressed the summer air. It felt as though time had slowed, as each leaf moved its own way through the pageant of life to stay perfect forever.

Just then the earth shook. The entire earth shook. A large rock nearby unsettled itself and nearly rolled over on me making me recoil in horror. Just as I craned to try and see what was going on an avalanche of dirt and leaves thundered on top of me. I looked down and there was a part of my bottom completely gone. I felt cold all over. Everything that was stable before was now in motion. Only the air seemed the same. Suddenly, from the sky came a silvery curve, all light and shine that took some more of my lower half off. I kept writhing in a kind of pathetic dance of evasion.

What's this? The earthquake has subsided! Thank the family, the sky.

In a flash my remaining body was squeezed and pulled from the earth by some mysterious force elongating my shape, yet I was not released. Air rushed by as I gained speed, still clasped between two enormous pink pinchers. I braced for the worst. Just then a deluge of rain or water hit me and all remaining earth was gone. After another floppy flight between the pink clamps I was released, apparently above an ocean of some kind, where gravity thankfully pulled me to the bottom. Not normal gravity though, or at least any I had ever noticed before. This was a buoyant suspension in water I believe. Thankfully, I was no longer being squeezed to near death by the pink pinchers. There were, however, other creatures flowing by, creatures with very large eyes. In some cases the diameter of their eyes was that of my entire body. But they didn't bother me. They floated by me from time to time in a dream world of existence.

My body began to lose its color the longer I stayed in the liquid. And my injury healed, though the creatures swimming by kept bumping me with their mouths. It was startling every time to see them approach but they only succeeded in propelling me around the ocean from time to time. Ultimately, I settled to the bottom of the place in relative safety, though I could not move myself to propel in any normal way. My customary movements from before, before the earthquake and the travel, did not now yield the same reactions in this liquid world.

The pink pinchers have unfortunately returned and this time they have plucked me instantly and without the least preface from the watery bottom of peering eyeballs. Liquid quickly dripped off my body, the feeling of air again chilled my form, and an eternity of bouncing earthquakes kept pounding nearby. Finally came my release into the air, with enough force on my form to distort my shape into impossibilities.

Space flight is indeed weightless. Computed as a fraction of my overall lifetime, I have been flying a small percentage of the time, and the verdure, the tempermanent green, past which I now project myself is but a thousandth of the complete sensation. The primary sense, is no sense, it is non sense. I have never flown before, though I have sensed that others in my family have been plucked out of their reveries and theretofore levitated somehow across space and time. This is a first for me and perhaps for our family in this part of the world. I am no follower, but I would like to live long enough to understand what is happening to me.

Landing! The top of my form brushed some branches and leaves a millisecond of sensation before I returned to the beloved, the predictable Earth. Now on familiar footing so to speak, I quickly moved away among the plants.

"Hey Mom. You know that worm I dug out of the asparagus patch yesterday? I put him in the aquarium and nobody ate him. So I just threw him off the back deck."

The Counter

It was late 1939. It was New Orleans. It was also somewhat unusual for a pregnant, well-to-do British lady and her relatively new husband to be bouncing along the countryside outside town in a new 1940 Ford. But they were an unusual couple. Their trip from the family home in London had a specific mission. The primary mission, other than to marvel at all things American, was to scout for possible new investments for the family fortune. Certainly a monumental fortune it was, in the extreme. It was meant to be a vacation of sorts, before the arrival of the baby. And with several months left until delivery, no problems were anticipated.

They had spent several weeks sightseeing, since arriving in New Orleans, riding the trolleys around town, visiting historic buildings and evaluating tracts of land. Along the way they had discussed at some length possible names for the baby. There was a decision, that if a girl arrived, she would be named after Harriet Barington, the paternal grandmother. But for a male name there was still ample discussion underway.

"I do like both names from your father's side. Stanley or even Manley are both good names," said the young wife as she unconsciously rubbed her hand back and forth on her round, protruding front. "And grandfather's middle name of Ransford is not bad. What if we combined the two? How about Stanford, or Manford, for that matter?"

The young prospective father driving the car smiled and said: "You have done it again my love, by putting your own creative mix on things, and running it up the flagpole so to speak, you have given us something quite new. I absolutely love both names. And I love you. Now all we will have to do is decide which of them to use, when and if it is a young boy."

"Linwood, could we slow down a bit? I don't feel a bit as I should like," said Christian Barington to her husband. The use of his complete name lended import to her request.

"She does look awfully pale, white as a sheet in fact," he thought. Linny, as he was normally addressed, slowed the car to take a better look toward his lady. It was autumn and the countryside was grey, as was the light on her face. Christian leaned her head to the side and rested it against the car window, closing her eyes. A slight sigh escaped her lips.

Christian found it impossible to get comfortable. She was at that time almost seven months pregnant and increasingly agitated. They had decided to go ahead and make the trip to America by estimating they would be back in Britain in plenty of time before the baby arrived.

"My stomach doesn't feel at all right dear," she said.

"Allow me, my love," Linny whispered, "to stop at the very next opportunity and we will attempt to freshen up a bit. That might help."

"Mmm...Maybe," she moaned.

On the drive toward the next town, a place called Hunterville, in Mississippi, they stopped at Mitchell's one-room store out by the lake, bought two Dr Pepper sodas to drink, and sat on the wooden bench out front. There were beautiful green fields all around and a small church in the distance, with a graveyard to the side, a place called Windy Hill. A black bird was in the tree overhead slowly cawing some inexplicable, strangely ominous utterance. By the store was the family home of the Mitchells, owners of the store and land. Linny sipped his drink and watched his wife Christian. The store had been formed out of rough-cut planks from the sawmill, with no insulation or other fineries. A big sign stood above the inside of the door: 'Swisher Sweets Sold Here', showing the small cigarillos in a pack. Hanging on the walls were kitchen items, hardware parts, and around the whole room were various kinds of candies, even some toys.

"I am going to go back in and get some saltines or something. Maybe that will settle your stomach dear." And he went to see what the large lady therein could offer.

From inside, Linny and the lady in the store heard the sound of a breaking glass bottle out front, and looked to see what was going on. They could see nothing, not even Christian. Linny rushed out to find Christian leaning over the plank bench, vomiting into the grass.

"Help me! Now!" she whispered, and continued bending over the edge of the bench.

She wretched again several times, but to no other production. It was the same sort of spasmodic twitch a severe case of food poisoning produces.

Myrtle Mitchell stepped out the front screen door of the store, slowly, closely watching Christian, then quickened her pace when she saw what was occurring.

"Good Lord!" she said, bending down to help Christian lift up a bit. "This girl needs some help. May be the baby's comin'. Tell you what, let's get her over to my porch at the house and call Doc G." Doctor Gilson was the one and only doctor in Hunterville, the county seat, about eight miles away.

Linny picked Christian up and walked across the country road next to Myrtle toward the house. Just as they reached the chairs on the front porch Christian began moaning with a strange sound not unlike an animal in heat. Linny put her down in the chair on the porch while Myrtle went in through the screen door toward the telephone in the hall.

"Agnes, you're gonna have to get off the line if you don't mind. We have to get Doc G on the phone and see about this young lady here from the store. I think she is about to have her baby." Myrtle knew her neighbor on the party line and had to get her to hang up so she could try and get Doc G downtown at the hospital.

"FLeetwood 4627 please Mam," said Myrtle to the operator. "Need to get Doc G on the line. We have a young'un here about to pop her baby out, from the looks of it. Gonna try and make her comfortable. She got real sick over at the store."

"Okay Myrtle, but I happen to know Doc G is all the way outside town the other way with old lady Ransom just now. I took that call," said the operator.

"Well, hell's bells," said Myrtle. "Tell you what. We can call him back in a few minutes. Gonna try and make this girl more comfy. Maybe put her in the tub or so, to relax her. Could you try and get Doc G and call me back?"

"Sure," said the operator, and they hung up.

Meanwhile, Christian looked as though she had physically diminished compared to the size of the chair. She was slumping, almost curling up.

Myrtle took charge. "Let's get her in the bathtub and see if we can make her feel a bit better while we are trying to get the doctor on the line. I'll get the water in the tub and let you know."

In a few minutes, Myrtle called out: "Bring her on in here. This should help her feel better." They undressed her and put her in the tub, where she did relax for a few minutes.

All of a sudden, Christian started vomiting again, this time in the tub as blood began to color the water.

"We have to get her out of here and to the hospital now," Myrtle said quickly. "Get her wrapped up and let's get her in your car."

Linny brought the car up to the porch as Myrtle wrapped Christian in a large towel and sheet. They put her on the back seat, with Myrtle holding her hand.

"Get back on the road and let's get to the hospital," Myrtle commanded. "Go up to that turn, go right and then the next left. Stay on that for about three miles."

Linny was worried, and driving faster than he should have. They came upon a pickup truck by the side of the road, where a police car was checking the license. Linny pulled over, got out quickly, and asked the officer to help them get to the hospital. They both returned to their cars, left the truck sitting there and headed to town with lights flashing and the siren screaming.

Christian's face had the pallor of death by the time they reached the hospital off main street by the courthouse. She looked as though constructed from gray clay. It was quiet on the street when they arrived except for a couple of people talking out front of the courthouse. Linny and Myrtle got her out of the car and nurses took her to the emergency room. Almost immediately the consensus was she was in labor, and was going to have the child imminently, at about almost three months prematurely. The situation was getting more critical with each passing second.

"We have blood pressure rising quickly," said the older nurse, with agitation. "We have to do something. Have we heard from Doctor Gilson yet?"

"On the way!" said the young intern doctor, looking frightened as a startled cat. He was unsure what to do, never having been in a situation of this gravity by himself. He wanted to help, to use his wits, but fear froze him from action.

"Blood pressure now critical, doctor," said the nurse. "We may have to do a

C-section to save her life. Let's get her situated."

"The operator just called and said Doc G won't be here for another twenty minutes or so. He just left Lewiston," said the front desk receptionist, who had opened the emergency room door to update those inside.

The intern, almost against his will, had finally made a decision.

"Let's go ahead with the C section," Doctor Howard finally said, and they proceeded to clean Christian up and arrange the surgical instruments.

The procedure went tolerably well once the initial shock of making an actual incision was over. The nurse was exemplary, the result was a tiny baby boy pulled from the mother. The umbilical cord was cut and the boy handed to the second nurse in the room. The tiny creature was breathing but its movements so small they were barely noticeable.

"Doctor Howard, we have another," said the nurse and they pulled a second baby boy from the mother.

"We are losing blood pressure on the mother, doctor," said the head nurse. "She is critical."

Just then Doctor Gilson arrived and immediately saw the situation, the problem, and the impending demise of the mother. By the time the elderly doctor reached the mother, she had no detectable pulse. She could not be revived. It was final.

Young Doctor Howard hurriedly apprised Doctor Gilson about the twin boys. Both were still alive, but very seriously premature.

"Get them both under oxygen immediately," urged the elder doctor, "with monitoring of respiration, and some positive pressure of the oxygen."

The apparatus was set up for both boys and the oxygen started. They appeared to breathe less laboriously and became more comfortable. Once the twins were stabilized both doctors went into the hall where Linny was on his feet, with a very concerned look on his face.

"I heard the emergency call. What has happened?" Linny questioned.

Doctor Howard spoke first, with a solemn demeanor, "I am so sorry, but your wife did not survive the births. We did all we possibly could. The situation was critical even before she arrived as you know, and we did our very best. I am so sorry."

There was abject fear in Linny's eyes. There was total disbelief.

"No! You are mistaken. We just arrived. There is no possibility you are right. It simply cannot be true. What? Births? More than one?"

"We are both so very sorry," said Doctor Gilson. "I assure you we did all there was to do. Christian didn't live through the delivery of the second boy.

The boys themselves are in danger as they are very premature. All efforts are being taken that may help them both survive, and of course we will update you with any changes. At the moment we must get back to the patients. Please accept our deepest sympathies."

Myrtle Mitchell was at the end of the hall talking with the receptionist and overheard the news. At once she walked down to the two men with tears in her eyes. "I am so sorry. If there is anything I can do..." and Linny groaned, looking distractedly out the window.

Linny didn't utter a sound for half an hour. And then, without realizing Myrtle was still next to him he stirred.

"Stanford and Manford Barington, they will be named, with the middle name of Christian, for the both of them, for their mother," he said. "We decided on those given names yesterday, and there is nothing that can change that," Linny said to Myrtle, without looking at her.

As the reality of that final day slowly illuminated Linny's consciousness, he at last allowed himself an exhalation, a refreshment of breath, though any actual respite was threatened by encroaching reality, a reality of obligations, questions, responsibilities, not unlike the wariness of a bird in a tree or a cat on the ground. Reality alerts the wary. At that moment, Linny would have preferred to have been back at their country house in England, discussing the fine points of an after-dinner port selection, or a new 1941 automobile design. He felt as if there were to be no life without Christian. The sound of a biplane hummed by and aroused him from his absence.

Within days Linwood Barington had arranged for the funeral and internment of his beloved wife Christian Catherine Barington not far from the store where they had stopped for drinks several days before. The cemetery situated itself by Windy Hill where there were some beautiful turn-of-the-century houses and horse farms.

It was a bucolic, memorable setting entirely fitting for those still among the living to imagine those lying still for all eternity.

Myrtle was instrumental in helping Linny with arrangements, and in fact had come under the general employ of the Barington family to assist with innumerable details. At first, the plan was to help in local logistics of working with the hospital to ensure the news about the twins was transmitted accordingly, but almost immediately, it was evident that Linny did not feel a connection to the twin boys. He may in fact have felt animosity toward them for technically causing his wife's demise.

The boys were not normal. It was apparent. One of them, Manford as he was named, did not respond to the light when switched on directly above him. The other boy, Stanford, kept grasping for any articles within his reach to move them into a physical line.

It was not known at that time, but the introduction of pure oxygen, under pressure, especially to newborns, to prematures, exhibits extremely negative side effects. The results are as permanent as truth. Toxicity on parts of the central nervous system, does systemic damage. One common result is retinal damage, with the twitching and convulsions of the newborn often mistaken for basic discomfort. The destruction of neurons in the central nervous system can happen while the baby is smiling at the attendant from under the oxygen tent, even as some of their talents are extinguished forever. It is an insidious manifestation of negatechnology.

Manford, Manny, was blinded by the oxygen at birth and retarded for life. He was institutionalized until he died thirty-seven years later. He technically never left the hospital after birth.

In some ways Stanford, Stanny, was possibly not so lucky. He appeared mostly normal those first days. Later on, he exhibited talents and traits altered for the rest of his existence from the oxygen toxicity. Loss of some of his normal features simultaneously rendered several alternating traits with almost astonishing abilities. Stanny was happy doing what he did, literally without thinking.

It is here that we finally arrive at the beginning of our story, a story of waste, of talent, and of chance. The stars had aligned, as if by accident, and they had created a dependent creature somewhat adjacent to the normal lineage of evolutionary progress. Accident altered the actor. Stanny conducts our story as with his life, the only way he knows as possible.

The oxygen under pressure had not damaged Stanny's eyes as it had irrevocably changed his brother. The toxicity had decayed parts of Stanny's brain. It had changed his cosmic balance forever. It had made him a wizard and a weirdo at the same time. He had talents, but his senses kept him from ever seriously capitalizing on his abilities normally. He was balanced but he was on the edge of consciousness, and it was thus from his very beginning. He was worried. He was just fine. There was never the possibility of telling the difference between the two, even for him. He could not tolerate change. But he was otherwise happy and content. He was a conformist to the norm, but in reverse. He didn't realize how dynamic the world wasn't. As human nature dictates, he assumed everyone sensed his feelings. They didn't.

Order was his talent and his curse. Numerical order, abstract order, distance, time, dimension, color: All these were the drivers of Stanny's synesthetic brain, where senses crossed inside his head to produce unexpected results. He heard the colors he saw, subdivided time into silent units, and remembered number sequences.

Stanny had an easy childhood with Myrtle. His father never returned, though there were several motions as though he would. In the end it simply never happened. Due to the demands of social life in England, Linny kept the money coming to Myrtle and her family, the ones taking care of Stanford the first. In an odd twist of life, it was the same house and store where his parents had stopped that first and last time that Stanny afterward called home.

School presented an exceptional resource for Stanny, as he reveled in the sheer number of stimuli from the people, the teachers, the places. It was as if a complex scenery of distractions paraded before him without the slightest cohesion. Though there were several attempts at returning him to classrooms over the years, he would leave of his own accord to find better things to occupy his mind. And he had many opportunities. Depth of view, and distance were especially intriguing. For example, a near tree in his view and a far house behind it presented a kind of calculable representation, with the relative distances and interrelations always numbers. Numbers were Stanny.

At first, the methods of interpretation in his gifted brain were absolutely abstract, but as he realized the simple measures of feet, and yards he would endlessly estimate the numbers of those units in a view, and in all views. The near tree became thirty seven and one half feet from him. The far house behind it another one hundred and thirteen. The relentless time and energy he devoted to estimating, and then measuring against his pace for the increasingly more accurate result, perfected his process over time. He became astonishingly accurate. Through his endless capacity for repetition he came to view the geometry of the world as an infinite assemblage of physical placements, of objects, many in motion, all worthy of view, analysis, review and update.

Then he realized the value of time as a variable of place. Time represented the ultimate challenge of interpretation, as distance seemed to become compressed or expanded by speed. A simple scene with a person walking down the street represented an opportunity to calculate distances, as usual, and then perform secondary calculations to estimate arrival times, passing other objects.

"Car approaching on the right; 437 feet away. Will pass me in 10, 9, 8, 7, 6, 5, 4, 3, 2, 1," he constantly calculated and corrected. At the same time a person walking the dog on the other side of the street was exhibiting similar opportunities for analysis, including the estimation of times when his subjects, as he thought of them, would pass interim objects in his view.

At one and the same time and in fact all the time calculations were underway for as many objects in Stanny's view as he could possibly process. It went on without what might be described as conscious thought. It was as natural as breathing to the young man. But that was not the ultimate fun. The ultimate entertainment for Stanny was adding memory to these observations, and he was amazingly good at it. After all, this was quite obviously his life's work, so it made complete sense for him to record and remember the statistics he was observing. He forgot none of the things he saw. Any time he found himself returning to a place he had already analyzed, he did not have to begin anew, he merely resumed calculating with his previous numbers, adding to them for that scene anything newly observed or refined.

Once, when a lady was on the corner by the Rexall drug store talking with the preacher, Stanny overheard her say: "That's good. Just have her call me. My number is Dupont 2311." Years later, just as the same lady by chance walked past him, he said, within his normal vocalization stream: "Dupont 2311," and in no other way greeted her.

There were instances of utterance, sometimes bordering on conversation, when conditions were right inside his mental fortress, where Stanny would expound at some length on his favorite topics.

"It is well known, the shape of the circle is very special. A pregnant woman approaches that shape when she gives birth. What is not so well known is the magical relation of the circle to the square. You can put a circle in a square, and you can perfectly fit a square in a circle. That is just how the cosmos started. And if you look at any harmonious pattern, from the scroll of a violin to the pattern of a pyramid, you can certainly find a circle that will fit inside it, and, and can repeat a square that will fit perfectly in that circle."

This kind of soliloquy could continue literally, not literately, for hours.

The kids at the high school felt sorry for Stanny, but could not engage him. One girl in the literature class composed what became known as Stanny's Sonnet, and put it up as a poster in the trophy room, though he was never there to see it:

To Stanny

There is no vision without light
No color without vision
No light without shadow
No life without oxygen
No sense without reason
And no art without perception
You see all

Stanny's synesthesia made him a natural musician, if not a traditional one. He was what might be termed an auralfactor. All numbers, all stimuli in fact, represented vibrational distances of sound in his mind, from low to high, with various aural colorations and timbres. With unconscious abandon, sounds constantly emanated from his lips as a continuum, a byproduct of the endless theater going on in his mind. To others near enough to hear, he sounded as though he was sometimes mumbling to himself, and sometimes whistling or humming odd sequences of sounds. On occasion it almost sounded like music, but that was rare. The sounds were his numbers. The numbers were his work. The counting was his existence.

Trains especially fascinated the young observer. He walked daily from Myrtle's house past the condensed milk plant by the tracks to the depot where the trains came by. For many hours each day he could be seen watching the trains, waiting for them, and whistling his numerimuse. He of course knew how many trains normally arrived or passed through, numbers from any of the cars he had seen before, and would blissfully wave to those riding by.

One day, a train stopped just before the station, with an open, empty freight car directly in front of Stanny. Without hesitation he climbed in as the train moved away from town. He ultimately arrived in Atlanta where he disembarked.

Several years later, as the sun went down on the coldest day of the year, with a forecast for a hard freeze forthcoming, several of the workers from the Atlanta homeless shelter rode out in a car to bring in any poor body needing warmth or food. Along the section by the church they came upon a haggard man talking vociferously on a piece of cardboard the size of a cell phone...

"Yes. Yes. I will get right on that the first thing in the morning. Shouldn't be a problem. Tell you what, let's get there a bit early to prepare," the man said. His face was red and ruddy from extended exposure. His hair had a reddish tint, as did his long beard. He did not acknowledge the car pulling up beside him, just the opposite. He was whistling an odd tune while intermittently saying words normally and then in reverse. "Exit; Tixe. Notwithstanding; Gnidnatshtiwton. Good one that, and twenty-one distinct words can be extracted from it. Olleh; Hello."

"Excuse me sir," said the driver as he pulled up next to the man, then, noticing he recognized him from the shelter, addressed him by name: "Stanny! How about coming over to the shelter tonight? It's supposed to be a hard freeze, I mean deadly. You don't want to be out here tonight."

"And why not? You know, I need the air, and to tell you the accurate truth, there must be space for my mind. The same thing happened to my feet. Just as soon as I could find empathy with the inside of my shoes, I found it impossible to enclose these toes any longer in man-made structures. Out here I am able to envision, and enliven, the cosmos we are in, with an infinity of natural circles, without the human-made corners. Rooms are so confining when you stop and think for a moment."

"Well, at least let us give you an overcoat, so you can stay warm. Here, take this one," said the worker. But the offer was ignored.

Mr. Stanford Barington walked off into the night, whistling an odd tune, and was never seen nor heard from again.

Stanny was in the end at home with infinity.

Shoe In

Out front of the pasta restaurant several business people were arriving for lunch. A line had formed inside and the two taking orders at the counter were preparing for the daily storm of lunch customers. Usually, the place would get packed within a half hour or so. The young man at the cash register was blind in one eye, but he was glad to have the job, and always took great care to make sure the customers were happy. Nobody knew how he had lost an eye, but from the looks of him he had survived several serious scrapes during his life.

Outside, a homeless man was standing by the street. His shirt was dirty, his pants were ripped at the bottom, or more clearly, they had worn off. He had no shoes on. His hair was bunched up and it was obvious from his gaze he was not normal. He kept looking around as if he expected to see someone, but he did not move far from the parking lot entrance in front of the restaurant.

From his good eye behind the cash register the waiter noticed the homeless man outside, so he went out.

"You need to move over from the driveway if you can. We have customers trying to get in."

The confused man said nothing.

"Do you have any shoes?" asked the waiter?

"No shoes," answered the man, without making eye contact.

"Well, please stay to the side a bit and let our customers in," said the waiter.

The waiter went back in and resumed ringing in orders at the cash register. Every few minutes he would notice the man outside who was still not seated, and also not going away.

In front, the homeless man was staring at the same spot in the sidewalk, as if there were something there that startled him.

"Gimme' a second, I need to get something out of my car," said the waiter to the girl wiping tables down.

The waiter went out the kitchen entrance at the back parking lot to his car. He had a worn-out pair of running shoes in the trunk, which he grabbed and ran back in the building, briskly walking through and out the front door to the man, still standing where the waiter had left him.

"Here is a pair of shoes I had in the car," said the waiter. "You can have them if you want."

The man moved nothing but his eyes. His look was of extreme suspicion. The waiter put the shoes down next to the sidewalk railing and went back in to work.

After a few moments the man moved his head to the left and the right to see if anybody was watching, then quickly stole another glance at the shoes. He looked like a cat, afraid somebody might jump him from any angle. He even bent down a bit to get a different view of the shoes. Then he circled them again and again.

During the next half hour, as he circled the shoes, he started to comment incomprehensibly about them and to them, sometimes squinting to get a better look. He almost sat down on the sidewalk, but was still obviously wary of the situation.

The waiter came back out and said: "You can have the shoes, but I want you to get them on and get going. You're scaring off business."

The man said nothing. For another ten minutes he circled the shoes, finally touching one of them with the toe of his left foot. He sat on the sidewalk for a few more minutes, talking with the shoes, and bent down and picked one up, sliding his foot in the one that was tied. After several minutes he put his other foot in the one that was not tied, still not standing or putting his weight on them. After an eternity he slowly stood up, like a new doe with wobbly legs, finally putting his weight on both feet. He tried a few steps and then seemed to notice the restaurant where the line at the cash register had died down. He walked to the door and almost came in a couple of times, in the end opening the door and walking up toward the counter, making some sounds from some far away point in between language and growl.

The waiter came out from behind the cash register and said: "You can't come in here. You will have to leave."

The man looked confused, and amazed that he had not been understood. The waiter told him again, and opened the door for him.

The man went out the open door and walked on down the street, with one shoe tied.

Dimmer N Dammit

Homer and Nell were a kind of social fixture around the neighborhood, much like old Blue Hawthorne who lived around the back, but then they were not as stable as old Blue, either from a social point of view or for their housing arrangements. Nobody knew where they lived, but they were seemingly always walking around the neighborhood next to the road, sometimes hand in hand, she the plump middle-aged lady at almost that dangerous ratio where height approaches width, with eyes that showed a brain not exactly focused on reality. Nell's vacancy signs included letting Homer do all the talking, including when he would expound on why the word dammit had two m letters in it. Sometimes a rare moment would occur when she could be said to have suffered from some inexplicable form of inspiration. She would snap her consciousness into clearer view with her surroundings, and make what for her was a serious comment, thereby displaying inarguable proof of her limitless distance. She would then instantly retreat to that cozy place behind her eyes where she was mentally passive, but physically involved enough to be able to walk next to Homer. Such was the intelligence of Nell and her world where most of the time she dutifully followed Homer not so much to help him but because that was all she could think to do.

Homer, for his part, was the picture of a slender 1940's style man, complete with the hat, the glasses, close-cut hair and serious demeanor. No matter that the date was somewhere in the mid-1980s. Homer could have fit in just about any picture from mid-century, completely in context. He even had a kind of depression-era gauntness that when contrasted with Nell's profundity of rotundity made a comical combination of characters so distinctive that they were always noticed, and almost always commented upon.

It wasn't readily known where they lived. They simply were a part of the small town pageant of players, the personal landscape of other animals such as the old man next door, with the emphysema from long decades of smoking. With his oxygen tank, he kneeled down to the ground when he came over to chat during the day. I worked at nights so I seemed to attract all manner of others whose daytime clocks did not seem to tick at the same fast rate of the corporate world. But Nell and Homer were obviously very special. They could be seen any time of the day or night, walking together, with Nell either obviously covering in great detail some important point, likely with Homer looking straight ahead. He and his '40's look, would increasingly show he was exasperated with her and he would finally make a comment.

"Dammit Nell, let me think!" whereupon she would once again have the female sensitivity to be quiet and let him cool down.

On occasion, they could be seen carrying out odd jobs, always together, and mostly down by the liquor store or over the bridge by the animal clinic. They worked mostly on things that involved easy lifting, easy understanding, and a minimum of concentration. But they were always around, and in some peripheral way involved. When the new gardening store opened they were gainfully employed for weeks taking plants from trucks to the sales sheds. But that length of work for them was the odd of the odd job. While working there with the plants, a young college student on a summer job worked very well with them, the student later diagnosed with Asperger's syndrome. Either or both of our main characters could easily have been diagnosed with something similar if they had ever visited the medical community for any reason. But they normally didn't. Well, they did once, and that is how they arrived at my door right around evening meal time on a beautiful fall night, to explain their predicament. I had never once spoken with them before, nor since. They were going door to door asking for any kind of work.

"We can do things for you. We can work," said Homer when I opened the door. They were standing on the small porch holding hands. Nell was quiet. No introductions. No manners.

I greeted them and noted I had seen them in the area from time to time.

"We had to go to the hospital and now we need to work and make money. It will be important soon," Homer said simply. "And we can do almost anything, if you have something. We could start right now or come by tomorrow if you want. We had to call the ambulance last week after we were just playing around, with a Coke bottle. Not sure, but somehow we got it up my butt and couldn't get it out again. Damn thing went on up."

Nell nodded her head.

I told them I didn't have anything for them at the moment but if I came up with something I would find them and let them know.

They turned around and walked hand in hand back out to the street.

Toe Jam

The little girl was walking across the street when she tripped on nothing at all. Across the street an elderly gentleman stumbled at almost the exact same time. One never saw the other, but the barber in the upper floor cutting the nth haircut saw the entire thing. When his next hairy stumbled on his way to the chair he knew something was up. Though he cut the hair of that third sufferer surely enough, he could not help thinking there was a problem afoot, so to speak...

Next morning there was a story in the newspaper about the Mayor and how he had planned to give an address at the town square but he had tripped late the night before on his way to the bathroom and had cracked a bone in his leg. The truth was, he had not tripped at all, but had simply stepped out of bed and lost his balance due to some new sensation of his feet.

One by one, the stories started to come in from around the town. The school principal, who had not missed a day of school in thirty-five years, was out due to a scrape on her face, brought about by a nasty fall while negotiating the porch stairs to her car. The radio station in the courthouse was relaying these stories as they came in, and they were coming faster every minute. By ten in the morning, there were more than four hundred stories of walking, and tripping, and the various fallings down, almost all of which regarded feet of those who as recently as the day before had been completely stable, and problem free.

Things seemed to compound themselves as the reports came in. The real question was about malice. If this was some campaign about getting control of these people then it would have to be dealt with on some formal level. But if it was some strange anomaly, then maybe it would simply go away and life would return to normal.

On the slope down the hill from Main Street at the barber shop by the men's clothing store, there was plenty of gossip about how the effects of this could be perceived as some sort of directive from God. There was talk of putting something in the paper about it. The printing office was on the same street where the melting of lead was going on to set type for the daily blatt. Mostly the news was known to be truthful if only now and then useful. At any rate, the kids playing behind the Greek restaurant on Main Street, could tell something unusual was up. The conversation in the restaurant was more heated than usual, even for a Monday morning.

Word had it that there was some sort of strange virus going around that could totally alter the shape of a person's digits and limbs. Nobody had proof of course, but there was an expert, well, a reporter, from the Clarion Ledger newspaper in Memphis who interviewed several people and ran the first story.

There was no immediate solution in sight.

The schools had to be shut down, and the radio station went off the air just before noon because the only two people working there found it necessary to take all shoes off to make room for big toes that were getting bigger every moment.

No one yet knew there was an epidemic brewing, and it had nothing at all to do with money, or age, or any political orientation, or particular brand of God.

Once people started showing up at the hospital with their big-toe complaints the evidence started to mount. It could end up being more important to these citizens than world war one and two combined. At least that's what the conversation at the restaurant focused on.

People thought it was a pestilence of some sort, like lice. But they didn't really know.

Shoes started not to fit, which caused people to become self-conscious about their feet. A ghost could have walked through the town sans wardrobe and would not have been noticed. Such was the subjectivity of the townspeople at that time.

A university professor proffered the idea that there had always been down through time, the problem of gout, a problem related to eating too much rich food. There were recommendations of toe poultices and remedies, some involving the reduction of rich food consumption. But normally the common man didn't have to worry about all that. Such was the malady of kings past, and not necessarily the province of those following the latest fast food advertisement for culinary guidance.

There was a momentary scare at the Greek restaurant, well, owned and run by Greeks and actually called People's Cafe, that there was something basically wrong with the kinds of food the restaurant was creating. But in about ten minutes of discussion, also at the restaurant, it was decided and downright universally declared, that since there had been no such problems in the twenty years the restaurant had been there it was likely not a basic problem now.

But what was it?

Nobody knew. And the speculation exponentially increased until the newspaper finally printed unfounded fabrications, and the national news media arrived. There had not been this much excitement since the school board got caught allowing cheating on the standardized tests.

It must be stated, though there was no real information other than the symptoms noticed, a kind of consilience emerged where all stories began to coalesce into something cohesive. The cohesive story did not make sense. It went like this: Anybody in this town who had been around Main Street in the last couple of weeks was   experiencing an unmistakable inflation in the sizes of their big toes. Little people noticed it, big people, old people, basically everyone. Brothers and sisters all agreed they had it, but there was nothing else to be prescribed.

The little old man of a doctor for the town had seen hundreds of fat toes in that day alone, and he had no more clue of fixing them than anyone else. Even the short Korean lady who sometimes had strange herbs and spices to formulate remedies could formulate nothing that helped this malady.

Nobody had an idea.

Except Ramona.

Ramona had arrived in the town late one summer night on the steps of the church, as an infant in a plastic storage bin, with some paper towels wrapped loosely around her, one of which had, in very flowery script, the word RAMONA, all in capitals. It was no time before she was heard, found, loved, and had become a part of the town. Ramona had dark eyes and light blond hair, and was a force to be reckoned with. She was smart as could be, and did not let anybody or anything dissuade her from her gifted focus of purpose, which she always knew.

At dusk one day during the fat-toe malady, Ramona walked into the restaurant during dinner time. The Mayor was sitting there having his meal, wearing some old deck shoes that could not hide the size of his expanding bigger toes. He asked her if she had heard of the problem. "Yes, and I don't have it," she said in an uninterested tone.

The Mayor jokingly said: "And I suppose that's because you know how to get rid of it, right?"

"Why yes I do," said Ramona, looking around the room as if bored with the entire interchange.

"Well, what is the remedy then? If you can, why not let us know? We will be forever thankful," chided the Mayor.

"You must soak your feet in a mix of olive oil infused with onions, and the problem will go away," she said a bit louder so George, the Greek owner could hear it behind the counter.

"Wait a second there my little friend. You mean to say all we need to do is boil some onions in olive oil and put that on our feet and the problem will go away?" asked the Mayor.

"Yes. It is completely true," she answered.

"George!" the Mayor called, "could you possibly give me some of your olive oil here if you have some with onions in it?"

"Certainly" George answered, "just a moment." And the Mayor slipped off his boat shoes right there and put his clean dinner plate on the floor in front of him.

George came out with a refrigerator jar of olive oil and onions, and handed it to the Mayor. "There will be a slight charge for that you know, as it is a kitchen recipe," he said jokingly.

The Mayor poured some of the mix on his feet and almost immediately felt the swelling in his toes go down. Within ten minutes the toes were normal in size again and quite comfortable.

"This is absolutely amazing my dear," the Mayor said. "How in the world could you possibly know that this kind of mix would fix the problem?" he asked.

"I just know," she said with a slight shake of her head.

"No really," he asked, "how can you know such things?"

"The same way I know you will be dead by this time tomorrow," she said.

And he was.

Turn Off

The agreement was for the dad and the son to go to the coffee shop the next morning. They both always got up early, and had not been there together for months, ever since Moonbeam quit working the cash register to get a real job at a spa. She was interesting, a modern hippie apparently, and kind. So both the dad and young son were a bit sweet on her. But the months had passed, and with the spring warmth the attraction returned for sitting out in front of the shop with coffee and a pastry for the boy.

The shop was built out of an old house from the last century, with the front cleared out to hold various wooden chairs and benches. Most everything looked as if it had either been picked up at a garage sale, or had been constructed on the spot from pine boards. No two pieces in the room looked similar, including the rotund female working orders and the boy filling the coffee cups. Art hanging around on the walls came from local wannabees, with wishful prices to match. But it made it all feel like a very friendly home spot, unlike the chain-owned shop a couple of blocks down, where they could not seem to open early enough for that first cup.

Decades earlier, when the street was narrower, when horses pulled carriages down the lane to the trolley car station, there was more space in front of the building. These days there is only room for a couple of cars parked in front, and some chairs waiting for sitters. A small bowl of water expects a dog at any time to come by for a drink.

Across the street a new burger joint looks on to the coffee shop. In long times past it was a filling station, and before that a house on the corner.

The young boy of about ten held his father's hand as they walked up the steps into the coffee shop. The father was answering the boy about how lenses are used for headlights on new cars.

"Did you see the LED tail lights on that car parked ahead of us?" asked the Dad.

"No, I missed it," answered the young boy. His eyes were large, blue with beautiful wide pupils.

They both walked up to the counter where the pastries were under glass.

"Which one do you want son?"

"How about that one with chocolate chips?"

They grabbed their coffees and decided to sit in the corner table by the window in the front room.

On the window sill, just by their bench seat was a neon sign hooked up to a power strip. The sign was on.

The boy reached over and pushed the rocker switch on the power strip. The whole world seemed to flicker for a moment, with the early morning light flashing outside the window as if with heat lightning. The "OPEN" sign turned off; all the other lights in the room went out. All early morning sound stopped except for the distant sound of a streetcar one block away. A horse could be heard pulling a carriage.

In the room things had changed drastically. The worn wooden tables were gone, replaced by a parlor and furniture, with a sofa of red velvet, and two padded seats by the window. By the armoire in the corner was a calendar with the current year 1912 showing. On the table was a single candle casting a faint light into the early morning.

As the person in the back looked toward the one by the front window he saw a young lady. Looking into the reflection in the window the other person could see himself as an old man. Both the young girl and the old man had a momentary long pause, as if the sleepy blink of an eye had come over both of them at the same time. When they opened their eyes wide again, they resumed talking with each other.

"So you have turned off the electric light in the window," said the old man. "Makes you nervous doesn't it? You know, people have been using electric lights for enough years now and there have been few if any real issues. Just need to make sure not to tip it over. It's much like a candle in that regard."

The young girl looked at the man with big brown eyes and said: "You know, Grandfather, you have always been here for me, from when I took my first steps up until now. What would I ever do without you I will never know."

"Well," he said after a moment, "when I am gone you will at least have this house as long as you want to stay here. It will always be yours; it already is."

"Come Grandfather. It is time to say goodnight," she said as she took his arm.

They went arm in arm to get ready for bed.

www.ingramcontent.com/pod-product-compliance
Lightning Source LLC
Chambersburg PA
CBHW030617130626
46552CB00002B/611